For Laurence
~ C.L.
*For Diane, Grahame
and Amy*
~ G.H.

This edition produced 2007 for
BOOKS ARE FUN LTD
1680 Hwy 1 North, Fairfield, Iowa, IA 52556

by LITTLE TIGER PRESS
An imprint of Magi Publications
1 The Coda Centre, 189 Munster Road, London SW6 6AW
www.littletigerpress.com

First published in the United States 2001
as *The Magic of Christmas* by Tiger Tales.
Originally published in Great Britain 2000
by Little Tiger Press, London.

THE GIFT OF CHRISTMAS

CHRISTINE LEESON

Illustrated by GABY HANSEN

LITTLE TIGER PRESS

It was Molly Mouse's first Christmas. The sky was streaked with pink and gold, and there was a tingle in the air.

Through the window of a house something was shining and glittering into the night.

"What is that, Mom?" asked Molly.

"It's a Christmas tree," said her mother. "People cover it with shiny balls, lights, and stars."

"I wish *we* had a Christmas tree," sighed Molly.

"Why don't you go into the woods to find one?" said her mother. "You could make it look just as nice as that tree in the window."

Molly thought this was a great idea. She called her brothers and sisters together, and off they all scampered.

On the way to the woods, they came to a barn. The mice rummaged through it, looking for something to add to their tree. Under a big pile of hay, Molly found a doll.

"This is like the doll on the top of the Christmas tree in the window," she said. "It will be just right for our tree."

But the doll belonged to someone else.
"Grr!" said the old farm dog. "That's mine!"
"Don't chase us!" cried Molly. "I only thought
the doll would look nice on our Christmas tree."
The old dog yawned. It was true that sometimes
he chased mice. But because it was Christmas,
or because he remembered the Christmas tree
in the farmhouse and how he used to play
with the children there, he said the mice
could borrow the doll.

The mice left the barn and walked across
the barnyard, carrying the doll. They came
to the edge of the woods.
"Hey," Molly shouted. "I see something else
we can put on our Christmas tree!" It was a
gold ribbon, hanging from a branch of an oak
tree. Molly scampered up the trunk, took hold
of the ribbon, and pulled.

But the ribbon belonged to a magpie.
She had taken it to line her nest.
"Please don't be angry," said Molly.
"I only wanted the gold ribbon for
our Christmas tree."

Usually the magpie chased mice. But because it was Christmas, or because she had also been admiring the Christmas tree in the window, she let go of the other end of the ribbon. Molly took the ribbon thankfully.

In the distance Molly saw some shiny round things lying on the ground. They were like the shiny balls on the Christmas tree in the window. "Exactly what we want!" cried Molly, running to pick one of them up. "Now we have a doll, a gold ribbon, and a shiny ball!"

But those shiny balls belonged to a fox. "Those are my crab apples," he barked. "I'm saving them for the cold days ahead."
"We only thought one would look good on our Christmas tree," said Molly, trembling.
The fox sniffed. He chased mice most of the time. But because it was Christmas, or because he had never seen a Christmas tree before, he went back into the woods. Molly picked up a shiny crab apple and carried it away.

Twilight was falling as the mice went deeper into the woods. There, in the middle of a bramble bush, they could see a shining star and a dozen tiny lights glittering green and gold.

"Stars for our tree!" shouted Molly. "Let me get them." But when Molly reached into the bush, she found not stars . . .

but a collar, belonging to an angry mother cat.
She had her kittens with her and their three pairs
of eyes shone in the dark.

"Oh no!" gulped Molly. "I only wanted something
sparkly for our Christmas tree."

The cat pricked her ears. She always chased mice.
But because it was Christmas, or because she
remembered the Christmas tree in the cozy home
where she'd been a kitten, the mother cat slipped
off her collar. She let the mice have it for their tree.

At last, in a clearing in
the deepest part of the
woods, the mice found
a large evergreen tree.
"Our Christmas tree!"
cried Molly. They hung
the doll, the ribbon,
the crab apple, and the
cat's collar on the tree's
branches.

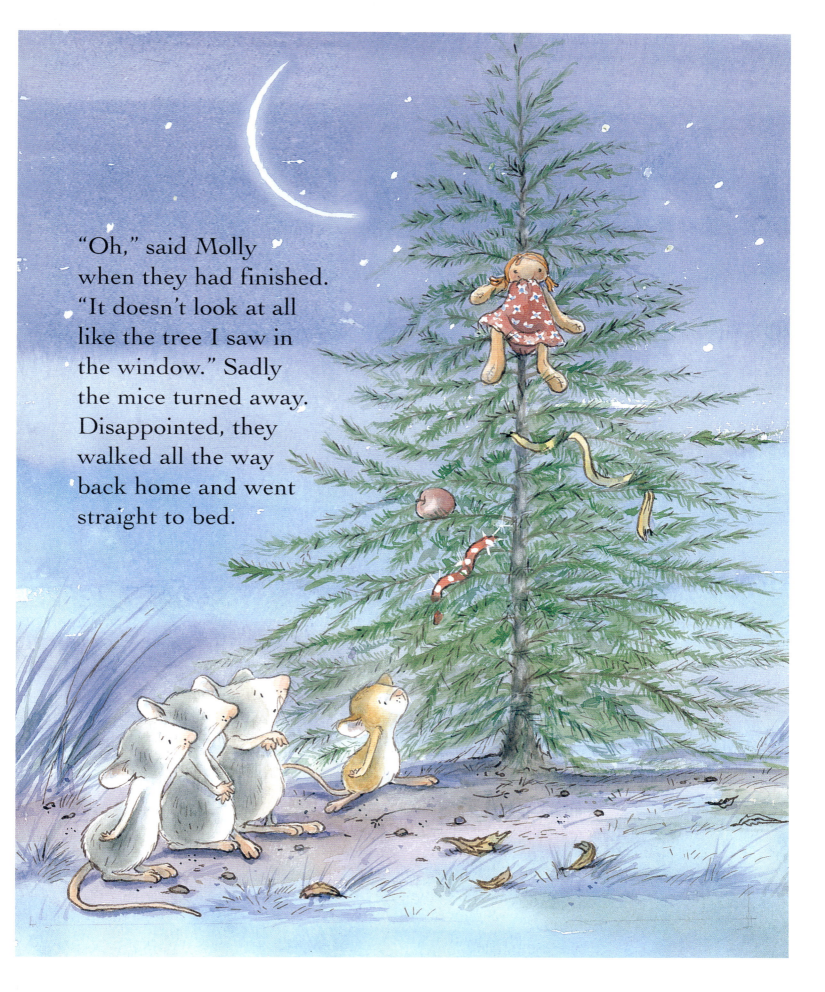

"Oh," said Molly
when they had finished.
"It doesn't look at all
like the tree I saw in
the window." Sadly
the mice turned away.
Disappointed, they
walked all the way
back home and went
straight to bed.

In the middle of the night the mother mouse woke up
Molly and her brothers and sisters. "Come with me,"
she whispered. "I have something to show you."
The mice scurried along behind their mother, past the
farm and into the woods. Other animals hurried on
ahead of them, into the deepest part of the woods.

At last the mice reached the clearing
where Molly's Christmas tree was.
Molly stood completely still. Her eyes
grew large and round.
"Oh, look at that!" she cried.

During the night the animals had all added
decorations to the Christmas tree. The frost
had come and touched everything with glitter.
The little tree sparkled, and even the stars in
the sky seemed to be caught in its branches,
with the biggest and brightest star right at
the very top.

"Our Christmas tree is even better than the
one in the window," whispered Molly happily.
And because it was Christmas, all the
animals from the woods sat quietly around
the tree, at peace with each other.